Max Makes a Friend

Grosset & Dunlap
An Imprint of Penguin Group (USA) Inc.

Based upon the animated series *Max & Ruby*
A Nelvana Limited production © 2002–2003.

Max & Ruby™ and © Rosemary Wells. Licensed by Nelvana Limited NELVANA™ Nelvana Limited. CORUS™ Corus Entertainment Inc. All Rights Reserved. Used under license by Penguin Young Readers Group. Published in 2010 by Grosset & Dunlap, a division of Penguin Young Readers Group, 345 Hudson Street, New York, New York 10014. GROSSET & DUNLAP is a trademark of Penguin Group (USA) Inc. Printed in the U.S.A.

The publisher does not have any control over and does not assume any responsibility for author or third-party websites or their content.

Library of Congress Control Number: 2009048148

ISBN 978-0-448-45430-6   10 9 8 7 6 5

"Max," said Max's sister, Ruby. "This is Louise's little cousin, Fred. Fred, meet Max!"

"You two can play with these toys while we make a sign for the Bunny Scouts Jamboree," said Louise.

"Share nicely, boys!" said Ruby.

Ruby and Louise got out their markers. But they only had orange, purple, yellow, and black. "I wish we had more colors," said Louise.

"Me too," said Ruby. "We'll just do the best we can."

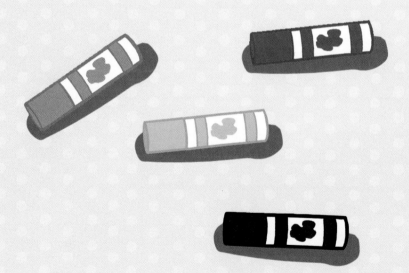

Meanwhile, the boys chose toys to play with.
Max wanted the dump trunk. But Fred
wanted it, too.
"Mine!" said Fred.
"Mine!" said Max.

Ruby and Louise went over to Max and Fred.
"Max, you take the ambulance," said Ruby.
"And Fred, you can play with the dump truck," said Louise.
"Share nicely, boys," said Ruby as the girls went back to work.

But Max did not want to play with his ambulance. He wanted his dump truck back.
"Mine!" said Max.
"Mine!" said Fred.
But then Max got an idea.

"Share nicely," said Max.
But Fred did not want to share nicely.
Fred took the ambulance *and* the dump truck.
Max did not want Fred to have both toys.
"Mine!" said Max.

"Boys!" said Ruby. "You are not sharing."
"Max, take the Chugga Chugga Choo
Choo Train," said Ruby. "Fred can have the
ambulance and dump truck."

Max went to get a caboose for his Chugga
Chugga Choo Choo Train. When he came
back, Fred had taken his train, too!
"Share nicely!" said Max.
But Fred did not want to share.

"Fred, you have three toys," said Louise. "Max has none."

"You are not sharing!" said Ruby. So Ruby gave Max his Jelly Ball Spitting Spider.

Then the girls got back to work.

"We're almost done!" said Louise.

"Yes, but I still wish we had more colors," said Ruby.

Max filled up the spider's jelly ball tank.
"Mine!" said Fred.
"Mine!" said Max.
But Fred pushed the spider's *SPIT* button.
SPEEEEW! went the jelly balls. And they
landed right on . . .

. . . Ruby and Louise's poster!

The jelly balls made huge red, pink, and green splashes!

Fred gave Max a turn. *SPEEEEW!*

Then Max gave Fred a turn. *SPEEEEW!*

Just then the Bunny Scout leader came to get the sign.

"What a creative use of color!" said the Bunny Scout leader. "This must have taken hard work!"

"Well," said Ruby, "we had a little help from the boys!"

"Sharing!" said Max.

"Nicely!" said Fred.